# Kathryn
## the PE
## Fairy

To Iona and Lowena

Special thanks to
Rachel Elliot

ORCHARD BOOKS

First published in Great Britain in 2014 by Orchard Books
This edition published in 2016 by The Watts Publishing Group

3 5 7 9 10 8 6 4 2

© 2016 Rainbow Magic Limited.
© 2016 HIT Entertainment Limited.
Illustrations © 2014 The Watts Publishing Group Ltd

HiT entertainment

A CIP catalogue record for this book is available from the British Library.

ISBN 978 1 40834 882 6

Printed in Great Britain

MIX
Paper from
responsible sources
FSC
www.fsc.org
FSC® C104740

The paper and board used in this book are made from wood from responsible sources

Orchard Books
An imprint of Hachette Children's Group
Part of The Watts Publishing Group Limited
Carmelite House, 50 Victoria Embankment, London EC4Y 0DZ

An Hachette UK Company
www.hachette.co.uk
www.hachettechildrens.co.uk

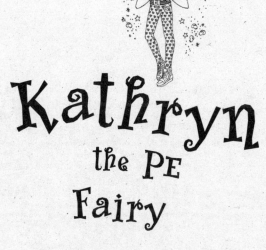

# Kathryn
## the PE
## Fairy

by Daisy Meadows

ORCHARD

**www.rainbowmagic.co.uk**

The Fairyland Palace

Fairyland School

Tippington Town

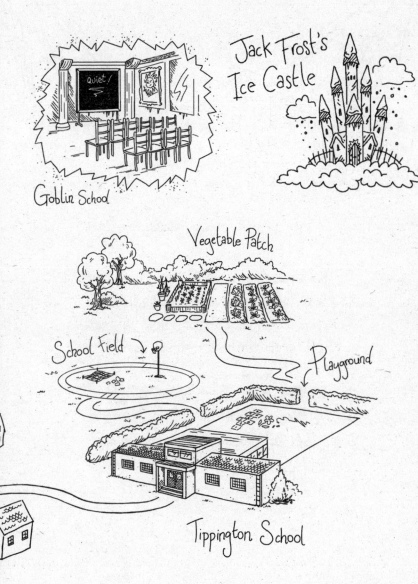

Goblin School

Jack Frost's Ice Castle

Vegetable Patch

School Field

Playground

Tippington School

Jack Frost's Spell

It's time the School Days Fairies see
How wonderful a school should be –
A place where goblins must be bossed,
And learn about the great Jack Frost.

Now every fairy badge of gold
Makes goblins do as they are told.
Let silly fairies whine and wail.
My cleverness will never fail!

# Contents

# The School Inspector

"I can't believe that tomorrow is our last day at school together," said Kirsty Tate. "It's been a wonderful week – I wish it didn't have to end."

Rachel Walker squeezed her hand as they sat next to each other in the school hall. The best friends had loved every moment of the past week. Kirsty's school had been flooded, so she had joined Rachel in Tippington.

"It's good that your school will be open again next week, but I am going to miss you so much!" said Rachel.

They were sitting with the rest of Mr Beaker's class for afternoon assembly. Miss Patel, the headteacher, clapped her hands together and everyone fell silent.

"Good afternoon, everyone," she said. "I hope that you have all had a good morning and are looking forward to this afternoon's lessons."

"Yes, Miss Patel!" said all the pupils together.

"Some of you have already met our school inspector, Mrs Best," Mrs Patel went on. "She is observing the school today and tomorrow."

A lady with a clipboard joined
Miss Patel at the front of the hall and
everyone clapped politely.

"I hope that you will all continue to
show Mrs Best what a wonderful school
this is," said Miss Patel.

Just then, Rachel and Kirsty
heard the sound of chattering nearby.
They peered along
their row, and
saw two
boys in
green
uniforms,
sniggering
and
muttering. The girls exchanged a
knowing glance. They knew that the
boys were goblins in disguise.

Miss Patel made a few short announcements and then sent everyone off to their classrooms.

"Look," Kirsty whispered, peering over her shoulder. "Mrs Best is following our class."

Rachel looked too, and saw Mrs Best a few steps behind them.

"She must be coming to observe our PE lesson," said Rachel.

"I hope that the goblins behave themselves," said Kirsty in a low voice. "It would be awful if they spoiled things for Tippington School."

Feeling anxious, the girls changed quickly into their shorts, T-shirts and trainers. Then they jogged out to the school field with their friends Adam and Amina and the rest of the class.

Mrs Best was waiting for them at the
edge of the field,
holding a clipboard.
Mr Beaker was
standing beside
her, and the
girls saw
him glancing
down at the
clipboard.

"Oh, I hope this
lesson goes well,"
said Rachel, crossing
her fingers. "Poor Mr Beaker looks
worried."

The goblins were at the back of the
class, mucking about. Just as they had
refused to wear the Tippington school
uniform, they had also refused to wear

the school PE kit. While everyone else looked smart in navy and white, the goblins were dressed in scruffy, bright-green shorts and stained green T-shirts. They were wearing green baseball caps to hide their faces. Kirsty spotted Mrs Best making notes on the clipboard, and her heart sank.

"Good afternoon, everyone," said Mr Beaker, putting on an extra-jolly voice. "We're going to do an obstacle-course relay, so I'd like you to get into teams of four, please."

"Will you two be in our team?"
Rachel asked Adam and Amina.

Their friends agreed at once. There
weren't quite enough children for
everyone to have four in the team,
so Mr Beaker told the goblins that
they could be a team and do two
obstacles each.

Mr Beaker led the children to the
course. It looked like a lot of fun. There
were all sorts of obstacles and challenges,
with bean bags, balls and cones laid out
in a different colour for each team.

"You have to decide who in your team
will go first, second, third and fourth,"
Mr Beaker explained. "The first person
has to balance a bean bag on their head
and weave through the line of cones.
The second person must throw the

netball into a basket. The third person needs to do twenty skips with a skipping rope, and the fourth person finishes the relay by crawling under a low net to the finish line. When each person finishes their part of the course, they have to tag the next team member as the signal to go. Do you all understand?"

Rachel and Kirsty nodded, feeling very excited. They couldn't wait to get started!

# PE
# Problems

"This is a tough course so it's important to practise first," said Mr Beaker. "I'll give you all five minutes to arrange your teams and then we'll begin."

Rachel and Kirsty's team decided that Amina would go first, Adam second, Kirsty third and Rachel fourth. Their team colour was purple, so Amina picked up a purple bean bag and set off around the cones.

"Wait!" cried Kirsty. "You're going the wrong way!"

But Amina didn't hear her, because all the teams were yelling at the tops of their voices. The bean bag slipped off her head and Amina picked it up again, but she had only gone a few steps before it fell off again.

"Noooo!" cried Adam.

Suddenly Amina realised that she was going the wrong way around the cones. She turned around and headed back in the opposite direction, and then the bean bag slipped off her head again.

Adam groaned and the girls bit their lips. They couldn't help but notice that the first goblin had already reached the end of the cones. Somehow he had managed to balance the beanbag on his cap without dropping it once!

At last Amina reached the end of the cones and ran over to tag Adam. He sprinted towards the bucket full of netballs and grabbed a purple one. He aimed it at the target basket, but it went straight up in the air and came down on his head.

"Ow!" he yelled.

He grabbed the ball and aimed it at the basket again. This time it flew over the top of the basket and hit the second goblin on the shoulder. He was fiddling with one of his trainers, and he gave a loud squawk. The netball bounced off into a muddy ditch.

"This is strange," said Amina. "Adam's really good at netball – he never misses a shot!"

The second goblin had replaced his trainer and thrown the netball into the basket on his first try, but Adam had to try six times before he succeeded. Pink in the face, he tagged Kirsty, who picked up a skipping rope. She was usually good at skipping, but after just five skips the rope got tangled around her legs.

*I can't have jumped high enough*, she thought. But when she tried again, she dropped one of the handles.

"You can do it, Kirsty!" called Rachel in an encouraging voice.

Kirsty picked up the rope to try again. But after fifteen skips the rope hit the back of her head and she lost her balance. She felt her cheeks going red. The first goblin was next to her, pulling at one of his trainers. Then he started skipping so fast that the rope whirled round in a blur.

"What's wrong with me today?" Kirsty muttered under her breath.

She looked around to see if the other teams were looking at her, but to her surprise they all looked just as confused and worried. Everyone was having problems with the obstacle course! One team was still on the bean bag section.

Kirsty took a deep breath and concentrated on skipping. This time she managed to reach twenty, although she tripped over her own feet when she ran over to tag Rachel. She glimpsed Mrs Best shaking her head and making more notes on her clipboard.

Even though the goblins had finished skipping first, they were both messing around with their trainers.

"It's lucky they don't have lace-up trainers to slow them down," said Kirsty.

Rachel and the second goblin dived under the low net at exactly the same time. Rachel dragged herself along on her elbows. This was something that she had done many times, but suddenly she felt as if she had forgotten how to crawl. Her elbows ached, and the finish line seemed to be miles away. The second goblin was already a long way ahead of her.

Suddenly Rachel felt a tug on her foot, and realised that one of her trainers was caught in the netting. Nearby, she could see other children having problems too. Some of them were still on the netball challenge. Mrs Best was shaking her head again and writing even more notes.

Just then the goblin scrabbled under the finish line and jumped up and down, cheering. Mrs Best smiled for the first time, and Rachel heard her speak to Mr Beaker.

"At least *some* of your pupils have satisfactory PE skills," she said. "Those boys in green are excellent."

Rachel looked at her foot. It was so tangled in the netting that she knew she couldn't get it out by herself.

"Sir," she called to Mr Beaker. "I'm stuck."

Mr Beaker came to help her, and Mrs Best followed him.

"It's almost as if they've never done PE before," she said. "What have you been teaching them?"

Mr Beaker helped Rachel to her feet, looking flustered.

"They have regular lessons," he told the inspector. "They *all* have satisfactory PE skills – I don't understand what's going wrong today."

"We're usually much better," said Rachel. "Please, will you give us another chance?"

Mrs Best looked at her watch.

"It will soon be home time," she said. "I will give your class another chance, first thing tomorrow morning. I hope things will have improved by then!"

# Gloating Goblins

Mrs Best strode back towards the school, and Mr Beaker sighed.

"All right, class," he said. "Let's tidy up the course."

Most of the children wanted to help, but the goblins just kept messing about, giggling and shoving each other. Mr Beaker didn't seem to notice.

"Rachel and Kirsty, could you straighten up the cones, please?" he asked.

The girls jogged over to the cones section and started to neaten them up.

"What an awful lesson," said Kirsty. "I hope that we can do better tomorrow – Mr Beaker looked really upset."

Rachel didn't reply, because she had spotted something very strange. A faint golden

32

glow was coming from underneath
one of the purple cones. She nudged
Kirsty, who lifted up the cone to look
underneath it. They heard the sound of
a tiny whistle, and then Kathryn the PE
Fairy fluttered out
and waved at
them.

"Hello, girls!"
she called.

She was
wearing white
jeans decorated
with red hearts, a
pink sports jacket and
a pretty pink ribbon in
her hair.

"Hello, Kathryn," said Kirsty. "What
are you doing here?"

33

"Queen Titania
was watching
your lesson in
her Seeing
Pool,"
Kathryn
explained. "It
went wrong
because the
goblins have got
my magical gold
star badge. I've come to
ask for your help."

At the start of the week, Kirsty and
Rachel had met Marissa the Science
Fairy, one of the School Days Fairies.
She had asked them to help her find
her magical gold star badge, which
naughty Jack Frost had stolen. The

girls found out that he had taken the badges for four subjects – Science, Art, Reading and PE. He was planning to start his own school for goblins, and teach them all about himself!

Without the badges, lessons had turned into a disaster in both the human world and Fairyland. But the worst thing was that Queen Titania and King Oberon were coming to look around the Fairyland School. Unless the fairies got the magical star badges back, the royal visit would be ruined!

Rachel, Kirsty and Marissa found out that Jack Frost had expelled two misbehaving goblins from his school and they had stolen the magical gold star badges from *him*. These were the goblins at Tippington School.

Rachel smiled at Kathryn.

"We've found the badges that belong to Marissa the Science Fairy, Alison the Art Fairy and Lydia the Reading Fairy," she said. "I'm sure we can help you to find yours too!"

"Rachel! Kirsty!" called Mr Beaker. "It's almost time for the bell. Please join the rest of the class."

Quickly, Kathryn darted into the pocket of Kirsty's PE shirt. The girls hurried over to join the other pupils.

"Before you all go and get changed, I want to talk about

tomorrow," said Mr Beaker. "There was only one team who managed to finish the course today – well done, boys."

The goblins sniggered, but everyone else looked very glum.

"It's really important for the school that

we do well in front of Mrs Best in the morning," said Mr Beaker. "Please could you all try to memorise the rules tonight, and practise at home if you can?

Remember, the first person has to weave through the line of cones with a bean bag on their head. The second person throws the netball into a basket. The third person must do twenty skips, and then the fourth person crawls under the net to the finish line. Don't forget to tag the next team member as the signal to go."

"We'll do our best to make everything all right tomorrow, sir," said Kirsty.

Mr Beaker gave her a worried smile.

"All I ask is that you *all* do your best," he said. "Now, I have asked today's winning team to give you all a demonstration."

Puffing out their chests and looking very smug, the goblins stepped forward. Rachel suddenly realised that if everyone was watching the goblins, they wouldn't notice if she and Kirsty slipped away.

There were some spare cones behind them. As the first goblin set off with the bean bag on his head, Rachel pulled her best friend's arm and ducked down behind the cones.

"This is our chance to find out where the goblins are hiding Kathryn's magical badge," she whispered. "Kathryn, could you turn us into fairies? Then we can watch the goblins really closely without being seen."

The fairy had poked her head over the edge of Kirsty's T-shirt pocket, and now she pulled out her wand.

"I'm glad you're going to be fairy-sized for a while," she said with a smile. "It means that I can give you a proper hug!"

# The Dirty Ditch

Rachel and Kirsty felt themselves spinning and shrinking, and when they caught their breath they were as tiny as Kathryn, with delicate gossamer wings fluttering from their shoulders. The three little fairies hugged each other.

"I'm so glad to have you with me," said Kathryn. "I wouldn't have any idea how to get my badge back by myself."

"Don't worry," said Rachel. "If we all choose a place to hide on the obstacle course, I'm sure we'll see something that will give us a clue."

"Good idea," said Kirsty. "I'll go under the net."

"I'll hide on the netball basket," Rachel replied. "What about you, Kathryn?"

"I'll slip behind one of the cones," said the fairy. "The first goblin has almost finished – I'd better hurry!"

She zoomed towards the first part of the obstacle course and landed behind a cone, making

44

sure that none of the pupils could see
her. They were all watching the first
goblin, who reached the end of the cones
and tipped the beanbag off his head,
laughing. Kathryn watched him run up
to the second goblin and tag him. Both
goblins bent down for a moment as if to
check their trainers,
but Kirsty could
see what they
were really
doing. The
second
goblin
tucked
something
golden into his
trainer and then
sprinted over to the netball challenge.

"Was that my badge?" Kathryn wondered aloud.

The second goblin threw the netball into the basket with ease, bent down to pull at his left trainer and then tagged the first goblin. Watching from the basket, Rachel could see that he had passed a gold star-shaped badge to the first goblin.

"Kathryn's badge!" she said with a gasp.

With the badge tucked carefully inside one of his trainers, the first goblin easily did twenty skips. Kirsty was hiding under the low net, and she saw him pass the badge back to the second goblin.

"That's cheating!" she exclaimed.

She felt so annoyed that she forgot about hiding from the goblin, and he

46

saw her as he dived under the finish line.

"Fairies!" he squawked.

At exactly the same moment, the school bell rang in the distance.

"Thank you for a wonderful demonstration, boys," said Mr Beaker. "Good luck tomorrow, everyone. Now hurry back to the classroom and get changed – it's home time!"

As Mr Beaker and the other pupils hurried away, the goblin swiped at Kirsty with his long, bony fingers.

She dodged his hand and zoomed away towards the muddy ditch where Adam's netball had gone earlier.

"Come back!" squealed the goblin.

He chased her, closely followed by Rachel and Kathryn. Kirsty flew as fast as she could, gasping for breath. If she could reach the ditch and fly over it, perhaps the goblin would run into it without looking!

Kirsty flew over the ditch, but the goblin stopped on the edge.

"I'm not getting my trainers dirty for a silly little fairy!" he grumbled.

Rachel and Kirsty darted up and hovered in front of him.

"We know you've been hiding Kathryn's magical badge in your trainer," said Rachel. "Please give it

48

back. It doesn't belong to you."

Kirsty flew over to join Rachel and Kathryn. They were all feeling worried. They had to get the badge back soon, or tomorrow's PE lesson would be a disaster. Suddenly, Kirsty had an idea. She nudged her friends and then smiled at the goblin.

"You were really good at the obstacle course," said Kirsty. "You must be a really talented athlete."

Kathryn looked a bit confused, but Rachel instantly guessed what her best friend was trying to do.

"I don't think he's that good," she said to Kirsty. "I bet he couldn't jump over this muddy ditch."

Kirsty hid a smile. The ditch was much too big for anyone to jump.

"Of course he could," she said. "Easy peasy!"

"No, I don't believe it," said Rachel, shaking her head and looking at the goblin.

He laughed and puffed out his chest.

"Of course I could jump a silly little ditch!" he boasted. "I could do it with my eyes closed."

"Prove it," said Kathryn.

The goblin took a few steps back. Then he squeezed his eyes shut, took a running leap and landed in the mud with an enormous SPLASH!

"WAHHH!" he yelled.

With filthy water dripping down his face and clothes, he squelched out of the ditch, his trainers oozing mud.

"That was your fault!" he grumbled. "You put me off!"

"Perhaps you should take off those muddy shoes?" Kirsty suggested.

The three friends crossed their fingers. Would their plan work?

# A Magical Inspection

The goblin shook his head. He sat down on the edge of the ditch and hugged his knees, looking very unhappy. Rachel, Kirsty and Kathryn flew down and landed in front of him.

"Kathryn, could you use your magic to make him some new trainers?" Rachel asked.

Kathryn waved her wand, and a pair
of glittery green trainers appeared in
front of the goblin.
They had zig-zags
down each side, and
tiny lights flickered
around the soles.
The goblin's mouth
fell open – he had never
seen anything so wonderful!

"Why don't you swap your old trainers
for these new ones?" asked Rachel. "I'm
sure they would fit you perfectly."

The goblin was already pulling off
his muddy shoes. He flung them aside
and pushed his enormous feet into the
new ones. Kathryn dived towards the
old trainers and plucked out a muddy,
slightly wet golden badge. It instantly

shrank to fairy size,
and Kathryn
polished it
against her
trousers until it
gleamed.

"Yes!"
cheered Kirsty.

The goblin
didn't even notice
that he had lost the
badge. He couldn't take his eyes off his
sparkling new trainers. Rachel grabbed
Kirsty's hands and they twirled around,
spinning into the air. Kathryn sent a
stream of fairy dust swirling around them
and they sank downwards, growing back
to human size. Suddenly they were on
the ground, still twirling.

"We did it!" said Rachel. "We got the last badge back!"

"You've both been wonderful!" said Kathryn. "Thank you from the bottom of my heart!"

She gave them each a fluttery kiss on the cheek, and waved her hand. Then, in a flash of sparkles, she had returned to Fairyland.

"Now there's just one problem left," said Kirsty. "We have to prove to Mrs Best that we can complete that obstacle course!"

Next morning, bright and early, Mr Beaker's class was out on the school field in their PE uniforms. Mr Beaker had set up the obstacle course, and Mrs Best was watching from the side. Rachel and Kirsty were standing beside the goblins, and overheard them muttering to each other.

"I don't want to do this any more," said the goblin with the new green trainers. "Without that badge we'll be as ordinary as these silly humans."

"Let's sneak away and bunk off," said the second goblin.

Kirsty leaned closer to them.

"Just give it a chance," she whispered. "This is meant to be fun – you don't have to be the best to enjoy yourselves, you know!"

The next half hour was filled with squeals of delight, laughter and cheering. It was a completely different lesson from the day before. Everyone did well on the obstacle course, and Mrs Best kept nodding and smiling. The goblins seemed to enjoy it too, even though they tripped over their own feet a few times.

"Good effort, you boys in green!" called out Mrs Best. "Excellent work, everyone!"

The class helped to tidy up the equipment and then went to get changed. Rachel and Kirsty were last to pile up their cones.

"That was brilliant," said Rachel. "I love PE!"

"PSSST!"

The girls looked around, puzzled.

"What was that?" asked Kirsty.

"PSSST!"

The girls looked down and saw Kathryn peeping out from behind the cones and beckoning to them.

"Kathryn!" said Rachel. "I didn't think we'd see you again so soon!"

"I've come to invite you to the Fairyland School," she said. "We're in the middle of the royal visit, and it's going really well – thanks to you! We think you should be there too."

The girls looked over their shoulders. The other pupils were walking away from them, and Mr Beaker and Mrs Best were talking to each other. Rachel and Kirsty exchanged an excited look. They knew that no time would pass in the human world while they were gone.

"We'd love to come!" said Kirsty.

A few minutes later, the girls were following Queen Titania and King Oberon around the Fairyland School. Marissa, Alison, Lydia and Kathryn were leading the way and looking very proud.

"This is our library," said Lydia, opening the door to a large, quiet room filled with books. "Fairies can come and read the books whenever they want. As you can see, there are always lots of pupils in here."

Lots of young fairies were curled up in squashy armchairs, reading, or fluttering around the enticing shelves. The king and queen smiled.

"You are running a very happy school," said King Oberon. "Every lesson we have seen has been fun and interesting. It makes *me* want to go back to school!"

Everyone laughed and the girls squeezed each other's hands. They knew that the visit was going so smoothly because the School Days Fairies had their magical badges back.

"Finally, we would like to show Your Majesties a gymnastics class," said Kathryn.

She led them all to the school hall, where the fairy gymnastics class was waiting. When they saw the king and queen, they began their synchronised flying routine. It was incredible! They twirled and spun through the air,

performing the same moves in perfect
harmony without a single mistake.

"They're amazing!" said Kirsty with a
gasp.

Just then there was a knock on the
hall door and Kathryn hurried to open
it. The girls saw her gasp and step
backwards. Jack Frost and a crowd of
goblins were walking into the hall!

# A Demonstration and a Display

The School Days Fairies were so shocked that they couldn't speak, but Queen Titania stepped forward.

"Why are you here, Jack Frost?" she asked in her gentle voice. "You have caused a lot of trouble for the School Days Fairies this week. I hope that you have not come to make more mischief?"

Jack Frost jerked his thumb over his shoulder at the goblins.

"These lot are so ungrateful," he complained. "I've been trying to teach them all about me and how great I am, but they're just stupid and they don't want to listen."

"The Fairy School has trampolines!" piped up one brave goblin.

"We want to play with all this stuff," added another, waving his arm at the gym equipment.

The School Days Fairies smiled at them.

"You're all very welcome," said Kathryn. "We love finding new pupils."

The goblins jumped up and down in excitement, and rushed forward to join the gymnastics class. Soon they were jumping on trampolines and leapfrogging over vaulting horses. Kathryn was a good teacher and she made sure that they all behaved well and took turns.

"Look," Rachel exclaimed. "I think Jack Frost wants to join in!"

The Ice Lord had been edging closer to the gym equipment. Suddenly he threw off his cloak and did ten somersaults across the mats without stopping. The fairies burst into applause, and Jack Frost grinned  and bowed several times. Kathryn came over to the girls, smiling.

"I think Jack Frost is finding out that school can be fun!" she said, her eyes sparkling.

"Thank you for bringing us here," said Kirsty.

"It's been wonderful to see you again," said Lydia, joining them.

Marissa and Alison came over too, and they all shared a big hug.

"Thank you again for everything you've done," said Kathryn. "We have to send you back to the human world now, but I hope we'll see you again soon."

The fairies waved goodbye. Then, in a flurry of sparkles, the girls found themselves back on the school field beside the cones. Mr Beaker and Mrs Best were still talking and the other pupils were still walking back into the school. No time had passed at all.

"Come on," said Rachel. "I want to enjoy every second of our last day at school together!"

That afternoon, all the Tippington pupils gathered in the school hall to present their displays. Every class had added different things. Mrs Best examined all the work and wrote lots of notes on her clipboard.

"Mr Beaker looks as nervous as I feel!" said Rachel, seeing the teacher biting his lip.

Maya, Dylan and Zac's model train was on display from the art lesson, along with book reports from the entire class. Rachel and Kirsty had added a picture of a plant from the science lesson.

As Mrs Best was reading some of the book reports, Kirsty looked around and nudged her best friend.

"Have you noticed that the goblins have gone?" she asked in a low voice.

"They must be back in Fairyland," said Rachel. "I expect they didn't like our school when they couldn't use the magical badges!"

At last Mrs Best reached the end of the display and turned to face the pupils. She looked down at her clipboard and then gave a big smile.

"I am happy to say that I am very impressed with you all," she said. "Your teachers are inspiring, your work is superb and your manners are excellent. I am delighted to announce that Tippington School is outstanding!"

Everyone cheered and clapped – even the teachers! Rachel and Kirsty hugged each other.

"I wish you were staying here," said Rachel, holding her best friend tightly.

"Me too," said Kirsty, feeling a little sad. "It will seem strange to be back in Wetherbury School on Monday. But it's been a magical time, hasn't it?"

"It's always magical spending time with you," said Rachel. "And I can't wait until our next fairy adventure!"

Now it's time for Kirsty and
Rachel to help...

# Giselle
## the Christmas Ballet Fairy

**Read on for a sneak peek...**

"It's Christmas Eve," said Rachel
Walker, gazing out of her bedroom
window at the snowy sky. "Father
Christmas and his elves are packing the
sleigh full of toys, the reindeer are getting
ready for their journey..."

"...and we are going to have the most
amazing day ever," finished her best
friend, Kirsty Tate.

Rachel turned and smiled at her.
The one thing that made Christmas
truly perfect was being able to share

it with each other. This year was especially exciting, because the girls had received a wonderful early Christmas present. Months ago they had entered a competition called Best Friends Forever.

Read **Giselle the Christmas Ballet Fairy** to find out
what adventures are in store for Kirsty and Rachel!

# Meet the
# School Days Fairies

Marissa
the Science
Fairy

Alison
the Art
Fairy

Lydia
the Reading
Fairy

Kathryn
the PE
Fairy

Kirsty and Rachel are going to school together! Can they get back the School Days Fairies' magical objects from Jack Frost, and keep lessons fun for everyone?

## www.rainbowmagicbooks.co.uk

# Giselle the Christmas Ballet Fairy

Meet Giselle the Christmas Ballet Fairy! Can Rachel and Kirsty help get her magical items back from Jack Frost in time for the Fairyland Christmas Eve performance?

www.rainbowmagicbooks.co.uk

# RAINBOW magic

**Calling all parents, carers and teachers!**
The Rainbow Magic fairies are here to help
your child enter the magical world of reading.
Whatever reading stage they are at, there's
a Rainbow Magic book for everyone!
Here is Lydia the Reading Fairy's guide to
supporting your child's journey at all levels.

## Starting Out

Our Rainbow Magic Beginner Readers are perfect for first-time readers who are just beginning to develop reading skills and confidence. Approved by teachers, they contain a full range of educational levelling, as well as lively full-colour illustrations.

## Developing Readers

Rainbow Magic Early Readers contain longer stories and wider vocabulary for building stamina and growing confidence. These are adaptations of our most popular Rainbow Magic stories, specially developed for younger readers in conjunction with an Early Years reading consultant, with full-colour illustrations.

## Going Solo

The Rainbow Magic chapter books – a mixture of series and one-off specials – contain accessible writing to encourage your child to venture into reading independently. These highly collectible and much-loved magical stories inspire a love of reading to last a lifetime.

www.rainbowmagicbooks.co.uk

"Rainbow Magic got my daughter reading chapter books. Great sparkly covers, cute fairies and traditional stories full of magic that she found impossible to put down" – Mother of Edie (6 years)

"Florence LOVES the Rainbow Magic books. She really enjoys reading now" Mother of Florence (6 years)

# Read along the Reading Rainbow!

**Well done – you have completed the book!**

This book was worth 1 star.

See how far you have climbed on the Reading Rainbow.
The more books you read, the more stars you can colour in
and the closer you will be to becoming a Royal Fairy!

**Do you want to print your own Reading Rainbow?**

1) Go to the Rainbow Magic website

2) Download and print out the poster

3) Colour in a star for every book you finish
and climb the Reading Rainbow

4) For every step up the rainbow,
you can download your very own certificate

# There's all this and lots more at
## rainbowmagicbooks.co.uk

You'll find activities, stories, a special newsletter
AND you can search for the fairy with your name!